This book belongs to

_____

_____

This edition published by Parragon Books Ltd in 2015

Parragon Books Ltd
Chartist House
15–17 Trim Street
Bath BA1 1HA, UK
www.parragon.com

ISBN 978-1-4723-8204-7

Printed in China

Disney · PIXAR MOVIE COLLECTION
A SPECIAL DISNEY STORYBOOK SERIES

TOY STORY 3

PaRragon

Bath • New York • Cologne • Melbourne • Delhi
Hong Kong • Shenzhen • Singapore • Amsterdam

Sheriff Woody was in the middle of another exciting adventure. He had made his way to the top of a thundering train, where he battled the villainous One-Eyed Bart.

But Woody wasn't alone – Bullseye the horse and Jessie the yodelling cowgirl were galloping nearby, ready to help. Still, all might have been lost without the swooping strength of Buzz Lightyear, Space Ranger! But the fight wasn't over. One-Eyed Bart and the evil Dr Porkchop struck back – attacking with their force-field dog and a pack of Aliens.

By working together, the unstoppable Sheriff Woody and Buzz Lightyear saved the day at last!

When Andy was young, his toys had enjoyed exciting adventures every day. Andy's imagination could take them anywhere: the future or the past; deserts, jungles or distant planets.

Andy loved his toys. And Woody, Buzz, Jessie, Rex, Hamm, Slinky Dog and the rest of the toy gang loved him right back. For the toys, being played with – and being loved – by a kid was the best feeling in the whole world.

But as Andy grew into a teenager, he played with his toys less and less. By the time he was preparing to leave home and go to college, the toys were very worried. What would happen to them? Woody tried to reassure everyone. Andy would just tuck them all in the attic for safekeeping, he explained.

But Andy's mum came into his room with another idea. She suggested that Andy donate his old toys to a daycare centre.

"No one's going to want those," he told her. "They're junk."

Inside the toy box, the toys felt hurt. Did Andy really think they were junk?

They were even more upset when Andy started scooping them up and dumping them into a bin bag!

But when he picked up Woody and Buzz, he paused. They had always been his two favourites. He looked back and forth between them, then made his decision.

Buzz went into the bin bag and Woody went into a box marked 'COLLEGE'.

Buzz couldn't believe this was happening!

Woody couldn't believe it, either. As Andy carried the bag away, Woody followed him into the hallway. Then Andy pulled down the ladder to the attic. Whew! Everyone would be safe after all.

But just as Andy started to climb the ladder, his little sister Molly called him. Andy left the bin bag in the hall. When his mum walked by moments later, she grabbed the bag and carried it out of the house.

She was throwing the toys away!

Andy's mum tossed the bag on to the pavement, by the rubbish bins.
The toys began to panic. "There's got to be a way out!" shouted Buzz,
looking around desperately. Finally, he had an idea: they could use
Rex's pointy tail to tear through the bag.

Everyone pushed Rex against the plastic as hard as they could,
but they were running out of time. "I can hear the bin lorry!" Rex cried.

Woody ran outside to rescue his friends from the bin bag and reached the kerb just in time to see the bin lorry pulling away! But then he noticed an upside-down recycling box making its way across Andy's driveway. He realized his friends had escaped under the recycling box and were now in the garage!

Inside the garage, the toys were upset.

"Andy threw us out!" exclaimed Slinky Dog.

"Like we were rubbish!" added Hamm.

Luckily, Jessie had a plan. When Woody reached them, she and the other toys were all climbing into the donation box for Sunnyside Daycare.

Woody tried to explain that Andy didn't mean to throw them out.
But the toys weren't convinced. Then, suddenly, Andy's mum slammed
the boot shut.

As they drove to Sunnyside, Woody told his friends that daycare was
a sad, lonely place. "You'll be begging to go home," he warned.

But when the car pulled up in front of Sunnyside, it didn't seem sad at
all. The building looked cheerful, and children were laughing
and playing outside. The toys could hardly contain their
excitement – maybe they would be played with again!

When they went inside, the toys got so excited that
they accidentally knocked their box over.

A crowd of daycare toys swarmed around them.
"Welcome to Sunnyside!" a big pink bear called warmly.
"I'm Lots-o'-Huggin' Bear! But please, call me Lotso!"

After everything they had been through that day,
the toys were happy to see a friendly face.

"Mr Lotso," asked Rex. "Do toys here get played with every day?"

"All day long. Five days a week," Lotso replied.

To Andy's toys, Sunnyside sounded like a dream come true!

"Now let's get you all settled in," Lotso said.

The friendly bear led everyone on a complete tour of the daycare centre.

By the time they reached the Caterpillar Room, their new home, Andy's toys were amazed. Sunnyside seemed to have everything they needed!

But one toy wasn't completely won over by Sunnyside. Woody reminded Buzz and the others that they were still Andy's toys. Woody wanted to leave Sunnyside and go home.

"We can have a new life here, Woody," Jessie argued. "A chance to make kids happy again."

"So this is it?" Woody asked. "After all we've been through?"

No one answered, so Woody walked away, alone, determined to get back to Andy.

Woody slipped out of the Caterpillar Room and found his way on to the roof. But a high wall surrounded the daycare centre and, for a moment, there seemed to be no way out.

Luckily, Woody spotted an old kite on the roof. Holding it above his head, he leaped off the roof and soared over the wall!

But instead of gliding gently down, Woody flew upwards on a gust of wind!

Suddenly, the kite broke, and Woody fell towards the ground. But his pull string caught on the branch of a tree, leaving him dangling in mid-air, and his hat fell to the pavement below.

At that moment, a little girl named Bonnie spotted him. She was just leaving Sunnyside to go home. Bonnie reached up, put Woody into her rucksack, and climbed into her mum's waiting car.

Woody was glad to be rescued – but he still needed to get home to Andy!

Inside the Caterpillar Room, Andy's toys waited excitedly as footsteps thundered towards them. Suddenly, a crowd of toddlers burst into the room. They tangled Slinky's coil, dipped Jessie's hair in paint and covered Hamm with pasta shapes and glue.

One of the toddlers threw Buzz on to a windowsill. He could see into the Butterfly Room … where a group of four- and five-year-olds were playing gently with Lotso and the other daycare toys.

Buzz wondered why Andy's toys had been put in the Caterpillar Room. The toddlers' play was too rough!

Meanwhile, at Bonnie's house, Woody was actually having fun!
The little girl had a great imagination and her toys were very kind.

But Woody discovered he was close to Andy's house and he decided he
had to get home. "If you guys ever get to Sunnyside," said Woody, waving
goodbye to Bonnie's toys, "tell them Woody made it home."

The toys knew all about Sunnyside. Long ago, Chuckles, a toy clown,
Lotso and Big Baby belonged to a girl named Daisy. One day, the toys
had been left behind on a trip. Lotso led them home, but Daisy already
had a new pink bear. Heartbroken, Lotso ripped off the pendant with
Daisy's name on it that Big Baby always wore. Eventually, the trio came
to Sunnyside and Chuckles was rescued from there by Daisy. Chuckles
had kept Lotso's pendant, and now he handed it to Woody.

Back at Sunnyside, the toys were tired and sore. "These toddlers!" exclaimed Mr Potato Head. "They don't know how to play with us!"

Buzz decided to talk to Lotso about being moved to the big-kids' room. But the doors and windows were locked!

Luckily, Buzz found one open window at the top of the door and he scrambled out to find the pink bear.

Buzz found Lotso's crew in the teachers' lounge, inside the top of a snack machine.

"What do you guys think of the new recruits?" Buzz heard someone ask. "Any keepers?"

"All of them toys are disposable," replied the toy named Twitch. "We'll be lucky if they last us a week!"

Buzz was shocked. Lotso had put Andy's toys in the Caterpillar Room on purpose! Buzz whirled round, anxious to warn his friends – and ran right into the gigantic doll named Big Baby.

Lotso came to speak to Buzz. The pink bear was friendly at first.

But when Buzz explained that he and his friends belonged in the Butterfly Room, Lotso stopped being nice. "Those Caterpillar kids need someone to play with," he growled. He wanted Andy's toys to stay with the little kids so he wouldn't have to!

Lotso strapped Buzz to a chair and prepared to switch the space ranger back to his original factory setting.

"Nooooo!" Buzz yelled.

When Lotso arrived in the
Caterpillar Room, Andy's toys
begged to leave.
"Here's the thing," the bear said, grinning.
"You ain't leaving Sunnyside." He wanted Andy's toys
to stay with the littlest kids because they played so roughly!
Then, suddenly, Buzz appeared and accused his old friends of
being 'minions of Zurg'!
Jessie and the others were shocked. What had happened to
Buzz? Lotso's gang herded Andy's toys into the room's wire
crates. Lotso chuckled and left, leaving Buzz to guard
the captives.

Woody was desperate to get home to Andy before he left for college, but he also knew he couldn't leave Buzz, Jessie and the others in Lotso's clutches.

So the next morning, Woody stowed away in Bonnie's rucksack and sneaked into Sunnyside. Woody's friends were overjoyed to see him.

"Oh, Woody," cried Jessie, "we were wrong to leave Andy!"

"From now on, we stick together," Woody replied.

Everyone knew that Woody needed to get home quickly so he could go to college with Andy. Luckily, Woody had a plan....

That night, the toys put Woody's escape plan into action.
Some of them distracted Buzz while Woody and Slinky snatched the
daycare centre's master key.

Mr Potato Head threw his removable parts into the playground,
where they attached themselves to a tortilla. In his new identity as
Mr Tortilla Head, he watched out for Lotso and his gang.

Jessie unlocked the door and led Andy's toys out into the
playground, while Rex and Hamm tried to reset Buzz.

Suddenly, Buzz beeped – and began speaking Spanish!

Woody tried to hustle Buzz along, but when the space ranger saw Jessie, he dropped to his knees. "*¡Mi florecita del desierto!*" he declared romantically.

"Did you fix Buzz?" asked Jessie, confused.

"Sort of," Woody replied.

Soon Mr Tortilla Head joined them as well. In no time, he was reunited with his old potato body – and a very relieved Mrs Potato Head.

Together, the friends creeped past Big Baby and across the playground, avoiding a spotlight that swept over the ground. Quickly, the group headed towards the rubbish chute.

Woody slid down the chute, then
called for his friends to follow. Soon
they were all outside, perched above
a big, open rubbish bin.
Slinky stretched himself across the bin
so that the toys could climb across to safety.
But suddenly, Lotso stepped into view.
"Are you lost, little doggie?" he asked with a
nasty grin. Lotso kicked Slinky's paws, almost
knocking the dog into the rubbish below.

"What about Daisy?" Woody asked suddenly.

"She lost you. By accident. She loved you!" He held up the old pendant that Chuckles had given him.

"She never loved me!" Lotso exploded angrily. "She left me!"

Big Baby's eyes filled with tears as he thought about Daisy. He picked up Lotso and threw him into the bin!

The daycare toys cheered. Things would be different at Sunnyside from now on.

"Come on! Hurry!" cried Woody, running. He could hear a rubbish lorry rumbling towards them!

My Heart Belongs To:

DAISY

The toys followed and climbed to safety on a wall. Then Woody saw an Alien caught in between the bin lids. The cowboy ran back, but Lotso reached up and yanked Woody inside! The rest of Andy's toys jumped on to the lid and tried to lift it, but the rubbish lorry lifted the container and tilted it upside down. Soon all the toys fell into the back of the rubbish lorry.

The lorry rumbled forwards, then lurched to a stop. More rubbish rained down on them and a TV landed on top of Buzz. Incredibly, the bump turned off Buzz's Spanish mode and he became his old self again!

At the landfill, the lorry dumped its load of rubbish.
Dirty and frightened, the toys struggled free.

In the distance, they could see the silhouette of
a huge crane. "The Claaaaw!" shouted the Aliens
excitedly, toddling off towards it.

Woody tried to stop them, but a bulldozer cut him off.
The toys were pushed along, caught in a churning tide
of smelly rubbish.

The toys tumbled down on to a
conveyor belt. Suddenly, a big magnet
began pulling metal from the rubbish. Slinky
was pulled up first – and he could see that his
friends were heading towards a shredder! The other toys
started to grab whatever metal they could find and were
pulled up by the powerful magnet.

Suddenly, a pink paw reached out from under a golf bag.
"Help me!" begged Lotso.

Woody and Buzz dropped back down and prized the bag
off with a golf club. They pointed the metal club upwards
and all three toys were lifted into the air, just in the nick
of time. Then they were tipped on to a new conveyor belt.

Everyone cheered to see that Lotso was safe. "Thank you, Sheriff," Lotso said humbly.

"We're all in this together," replied Woody.

Unfortunately, the new conveyor wasn't truly safe – it led to a flaming incinerator! Lotso spotted an emergency stop button, and the others boosted him up to reach it.

Lotso was about to push the button. But as he looked at the other toys, a cruel grin spread across his face. Instead of saving them, he ran away!

Terrified, the toys tumbled towards the fiery
blaze. It looked as if there was no escape. They
held each other's hands, together till the end.

Suddenly, a giant crane appeared from
above them. Its jaws opened, scooping them
up and away from the inferno!

As they soared through the air, the toys
could see the Aliens at the controls of
the crane! "The Claaaaw!" the Aliens
cried joyfully.

The Aliens set the toys gently on the ground.

"Come on, Woody," said Jessie. "We've got to get you home."

Fortunately, their neighbourhood rubbish collector was just climbing into his lorry. The toys jumped on board, eager to hitch a ride.

Lotso was going somewhere, too. A different rubbish collector had found him and happily tied the pink bear to the front grille of his rubbish lorry. "I had me one o' these when I was a kid!" the driver exclaimed.

ATTIC

Woody and the gang arrived home as Andy was loading up the car.
They had made it just in time!

Woody headed for a box marked 'COLLEGE', while the others climbed
into an 'ATTIC' box. Before they separated, Woody and Buzz shook hands.

"You know where to find us, cowboy," Buzz said finally.

Inside the 'COLLEGE' box, Woody looked at a photo of Andy with all
his toys and he suddenly had an idea. He jumped out of the box, wrote
something on a sticky note, and stuck it on the attic box.

When Andy returned, he was thrilled to see his toys! He'd thought
they were gone forever. Then he looked at the sticky note.

"Hey, Mum," he called. "So you really think I should donate these?"

"It's up to you, honey," she replied.

Andy loaded the box into his car and drove to the address written
on the sticky note. It was a small house with a little girl playing in the
front garden. It was Bonnie's house!

Andy pulled his toys from the box and introduced each one to Bonnie. And at the bottom of the box, there was Woody! Andy was surprised – Woody was supposed to go to college with him. But Bonnie recognized Woody immediately. "My cowboy!" she exclaimed. When Andy saw how much Bonnie loved Woody, he decided to leave his favourite toy with her, too.

Then Andy played with Bonnie and all his old toys. After so many years, Woody, Buzz and the others were finally getting what they wanted: one last playtime with Andy.

Back in the car, Andy
took a last look at Bonnie,
surrounded by his toys.
"Bye, guys," he said quietly.
Bonnie ran inside for lunch and the toys
watched Andy drive away.
"So long, partner," said Woody with a wave.
Buzz put his arm around Woody. Yes, their
life with Andy was ending. But their adventures
with Bonnie had just begun.

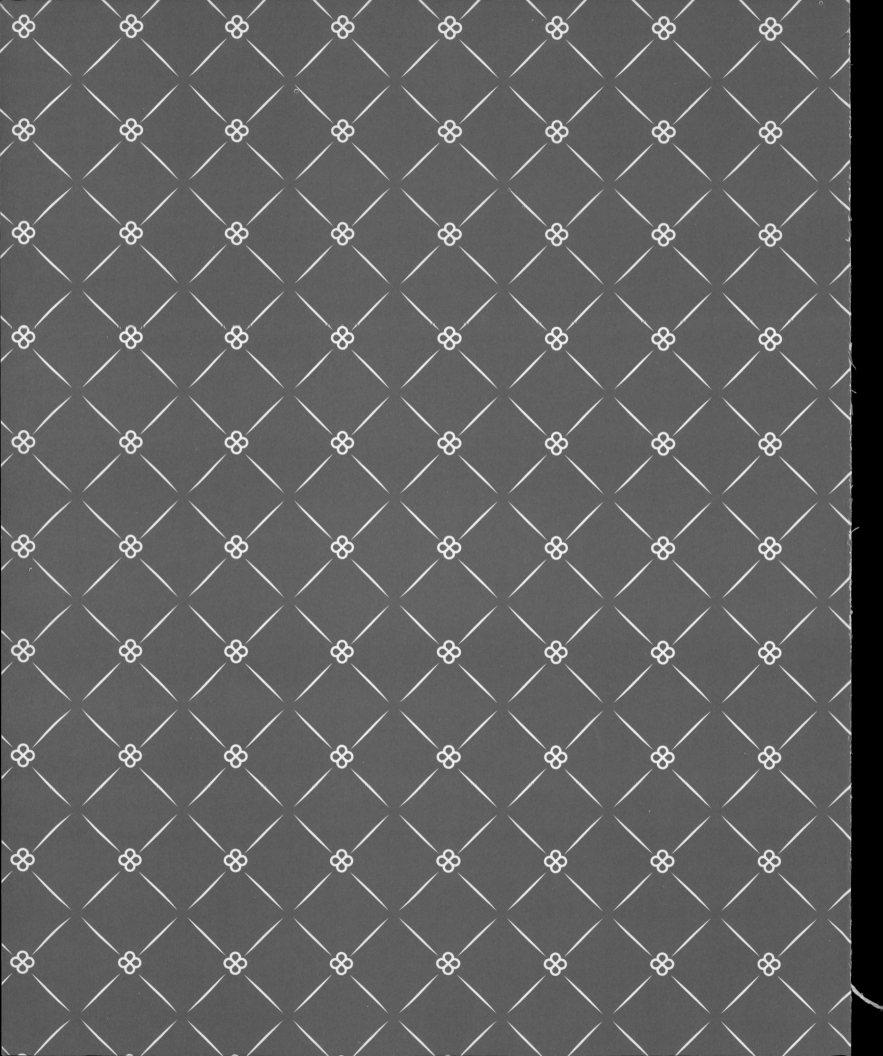